# the necklace

the necklace

# the necklace

### guy de maupassant

### gary kelley

design: louise fili

creative education
mankato

This edition first published in 1992

by Creative Education, Inc.,

123 South Broad Street,

Mankato, MN 56001 USA

Designed by Louise Fili

Art Director Rita Marshall

Illustrations © Gary Kelley 1992

Text translated from the French

by Artine Artinian.

Text reprinted by permission of Doubleday

Printed in Italy.

LIBRARY OF CONGRESS CATALOGING-

IN-PUBLICATION DATA

Maupassant, Guy de, 1850-1893.

[Parure. English]

The necklace/Guy de Maupassant:

[illustrated by] Gary Kelley:

translated by Artine Artinian

Translation of: La parure.

Summary: After devoting their

energies and income for ten years

to replacing a borrowed diamond

necklace which they have lost,

a woman and her husband learn

the irony of their efforts.

ISBN 0-88682-489-3

[1. Necklaces—Fiction.]

I. Kelley, Gary, ill.  II. Title.

PZ7.M44515Ne 1992

[Fic]—dc20        91-47913

CIP

# the necklace

he was one of those pretty. charming

young ladies, born, as if through an error of destiny, into a family of

clerks. She had no dowry, no hopes, no means of becoming known,

appreciated, loved and married by a man either rich or distinguished;

and she allowed herself to marry a petty clerk in the office of the

Board of Education.

She was simple, not being able to adorn herself, but she was

unhappy, as one out of her class; for women belong to no caste, no

race, their grace, their beauty and their charm serving them in the place of birth and family. Their inborn finesse, their instinctive elegance, their suppleness of wit, are their only aristocracy, making some daughters of the people the equal of great ladies.

She suffered incessantly, feeling herself born for all delicacies and luxuries. She suffered from the poverty of her apartment, the shabby walls, the worn chairs and the faded stuffs. All these things, which another woman of her station would not have noticed, tortured and angered her. The sight of the little Breton, who made this humble home, awoke in her sad regrets and desperate dreams. She thought of quiet antechambers with their oriental hangings lighted by high bronze torches and of the two great footmen in short trousers who sleep in the large armchairs, made sleepy by the heavy air from the heating apparatus. She thought of large drawing rooms hung in old silks, of graceful pieces of furniture carrying bric-a-brac of inestimable value and of the little perfumed coquettish apartments made for five o'clock chats with most intimate friends, men known and sought after, whose attention all women envied and desired.

 When she seated her-self for dinner before the round table, where the table-cloth had been used three days, opposite her husband who uncovered the tureen with a delight-ed air, saying: "Oh! the good potpie! I know nothing better than that," she would think of the elegant dinners, of the shining silver, of the tapestries peopling the walls with ancient personages and rare birds in the midst of fairy forests; she thought of the exquisite food served on marvelous dishes, of the whispered gallantries, listened to with the smile of the Sphinx while eating the rose-colored flesh of the trout or a chicken's wing.

She had neither frocks nor jewels, nothing. And she loved only those things. She felt that she was made for them. She had such a desire to please, to be sought after, to be clever and courted.

She had a rich friend, a schoolmate at the convent, whom she did not like to visit; she suffered so much when she returned.

And she wept for whole days from chagrin, from regret, from despair
and disappointment.

One evening her husband returned, elated, bearing in his
hand a large envelope.

"Here," he said, "here is something for you."

She quickly tore open the wrapper and drew out a printed
card on which were inscribed these words:

> The Minister of Public Instruction
>
> and Madame George Ramponneau
>
> ask the honor of M. and Mme Loisel's company
>
> Monday evening, January 18
>
> at the Minister's residence.

Instead of being delighted, as her husband had hoped, she
threw the invitation spitefully upon the table, murmuring:

"What do you suppose I want with that?"

"But, my dearie, I thought it would make you happy. You never go out, and this is an occasion, and a fine one! I had a great deal of trouble to get it. Everybody wishes one, and it is very select; not many are given to employees. You will see the whole official world there."

She looked at him with an irritated eye and declared impatiently:

"What do you suppose I have to wear to such a thing as that?"

He had not thought of that; he stammered:

"Why, the dress you wear when we go to the theater. It seems very pretty to me."

He was silent, stupefied, in dismay, at the sight of his wife weeping. Two great tears fell slowly from the corners of her eyes toward the corners of her mouth; he stammered:

"What is the matter? What is the matter?"

By a violent effort she had controlled her vexation and responded in a calm voice, wiping her moist cheeks:

"Nothing. Only I have no dress and consequently I cannot go to this affair. Give your card to some colleague whose wife is better fitted out than I."

He was grieved but answered:

"Let us see, Matilda. How much would a suitable costume cost, something that would serve for other occasions, something very simple?"

She reflected for some seconds, making estimates and thinking of a sum that she could ask for without bringing with it an immediate refusal and a frightened exclamation from the economical clerk.

Finally she said in a hesitating voice:

"I cannot tell exactly, but it seems to me that four hundred francs ought to cover it."

He turned a little pale, for he had saved just this sum to buy

a gun that he might be able to join some hunting parties the next

summer, on the plains at Nanterre, with some friends who went to

shoot larks up there on Sunday. Nevertheless, he answered:

"Very well. I will give you four hundred francs. But try to

have a pretty dress."

❧

The day of the ball approached, and Mme Loisel seemed sad,

disturbed, anxious. Nevertheless, her dress was nearly ready. Her

husband said to her one evening:

"What is the matter with you? You have acted strangely for

two or three days."

And she responded: "I am vexed not to have a jewel, not one

stone, nothing to adorn myself with. I shall have such a poverty-

laden look. I would prefer not to go to this party."

He replied: "You can wear some natural flowers. At this sea-

son they look very chic. For ten francs you can have two or three magnificent roses."

She was not convinced. "No," she replied, "there is nothing more humiliating than to have a shabby air in the midst of rich women."

Then her husband cried out: "How stupid we are! Go and find your friend Madame Forestier and ask her to lend you her jewels. You are well enough acquainted with her to do this."

She uttered a cry of joy. "It is true!" she said. "I had not thought of that."

The next day she took herself to her friend's house and related her story of distress. Mme Forestier went to her closet with the glass doors, took out a large jewel case, brought it, opened it and said: "Choose, my dear."

She saw at first some brace-lets, then a collar of pearls, then a Venetian cross of gold and jewels and of admirable workmanship. She tried

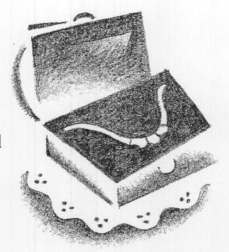

the jewels before the glass, hesitated, but could neither decide to take them nor leave them. Then she asked:

"Have you nothing more?"

"Why, yes. Look for yourself. I do not know what will please you."

Suddenly she discovered in a black satin box a superb necklace of diamonds, and her heart beat fast with an immoderate desire. Her hands trembled as she took them up. She placed them about her throat, against her dress, and remained in ecstasy before them. Then she asked in a hesitating voice full of anxiety:

"Could you lend me this? Only this?"

"Why, yes, certainly."

She fell upon the neck of her friend, embraced her with passion, then went away with her treasure.

❧

The day of the ball arrived. Mme Loisel was a great success. She was the prettiest of all, elegant, gracious, smiling and full of joy.

All the men noticed her, asked her name and wanted to be present-ed. All the members of the Cabinet wished to waltz with her. The minister of education paid her some attention.

She danced with enthusiasm, with passion, intoxicated with pleasure, thinking of nothing, in the triumph of her beauty, in the glory of her success, in a kind of cloud of happiness that came of all this homage and all this admiration, of all these awakened desires and this victory so complete and sweet to the heart of woman.

She went home toward four o'clock in the morning. Her husband had been half asleep in one of the little salons since midnight with three other gentlemen whose wives were enjoying themselves very much.

He threw around her shoulders the wraps they had carried for the coming home, modest garments of everyday wear, whose poverty clashed with the elegance of the ball costume. She felt this

 and wished to hurry away in order not

to be noticed by the other women who

were wrapping themselves in rich furs.

Loisel detained her. "Wait," said he.

"You will catch cold out there. I am going to call a cab."

But she would not listen and descended the steps rapidly.

When they were in the street they found no carriage, and they began

to seek for one, hailing the coachmen whom they saw at a distance.

They walked along toward the Seine, hopeless and shivering.

Finally they found on the dock one of those old nocturnal coupés

that one sees in Paris after nightfall, as if they were ashamed of their

misery by day.

It took them as far as their door in Martyr Street, and they

went wearily up to their apartment. It was all over for her. And on

his part he remembered that he would have to be at the office by ten

o'clock.

She removed the wraps from her shoulders before the glass

for a final view of herself in her glory. Suddenly she uttered a cry.

Her necklace was not around her neck.

Her husband, already half undressed, asked: "What is the

matter?"

She turned toward him excitedly:

"I have—I have—I no longer have Madame Forestier's neck-

lace."

He arose in dismay: "What! How is that? It is not possible."

And they looked in the folds of the dress, in the folds of the

mantle, in the pockets, everywhere. They could not find it.

He asked: "You are sure you still had it when we left the

house?"

"Yes, I felt it in the vestibule as we came out."

"But if you had lost it in the

street we should have heard it fall. It

must be in the cab."

"Yes. It is probable. Did you

take the number?"

"No. And you, did you notice

what it was?"

"No."

They looked at each

other, utterly cast down.

Finally Loisel dressed himself again.

"I am going," said he, "over the track where we went on foot,

to see if I can find it."

And he went. She remained in her evening gown, not having

the force to go to bed, stretched upon a chair, without ambition or

thoughts.

Toward seven o'clock her husband returned. He had found

nothing.

He went to the police and to the cab offices and put an

advertisement in the newspapers, offering a reward; he did everything

that afforded them a suspicion of hope.

She waited all day in a state of bewilderment before this frightful disaster. Loisel returned at evening, with his face harrowed and pale, and had discovered nothing.

"It will be necessary," said he, "to write to your friend that you have broken the clasp of the necklace and that you will have it repaired. That will give us time to turn around."

She wrote as he dictated.

At the end of a week they had lost all hope. And Loisel, older by five years, declared:

"We must take measures to replace this jewel."

The next day they took the box which had inclosed it to the jeweler whose name was on the inside. He consulted his books.

"It is not I, madame," said he, "who sold this necklace; I only furnished the casket."

Then they went from jeweler to jeweler, seeking a necklace like the other one, consulting their memories, and ill, both of them, with chagrin and anxiety.

In a shop of the Palais-Royal they found a chaplet of diamonds which seemed to them exactly like the one they had lost. It was valued at forty thousand francs. They could get it for thirty-six thousand.

They begged the jeweler not to sell it for three days. And they made an arrangement by which they might return it for thirty-four thousand francs if they found the other one before the end of February.

Loisel possessed eighteen thousand francs which his father had left him. He borrowed the rest.

He borrowed it, asking for a thousand francs of one, five hundred of another, five louis of this one and three louis of that one. He gave notes, made ruinous promises, took money of usurers and the whole race of lenders. He compromised his whole existence, in

fact, risked his signature without even knowing whether he could make it good or not, and, harassed by anxiety for the future, by the black misery which surrounded him and by the prospect of all physical privations and moral torture, he went to get the new necklace, depositing on the merchant's counter thirty-six thousand francs.

When Mme Loisel took back the jewels to Mme Forestier the latter said to her in a frigid tone:

"You should have returned them to me sooner, for I might have needed them."

She did open the jewel box as her friend feared she would. If she should perceive the substitution what would she think? What should she say? Would she take her for a robber?

Mme Loisel now knew the horrible life of necessity. She did her part, however, completely, heroically. It was necessary to pay this frightful debt.

She would pay it. They sent away the maid; they changed their lodgings; they rented some rooms under a mansard roof.

She learned the heavy cares of a household, the odious work of a kitchen. She washed the dishes, using her rosy nails upon the greasy pots and the bottoms of the stewpans. She washed the soiled linen, the chemises and dishcloths, which she hung on the line to dry; she took down the refuse to the street each morning and brought up the water, stopping at each landing to breathe. And, clothed like a woman of the people, she went to the grocer's, the butcher's and the fruiterer's with her basket on her arm shopping, haggling to the last sou her miserable money.

Every month it was necessary to renew some notes, thus obtaining time, and to pay others.

The husband worked evenings, putting the books of some merchants in order, and nights he often did copying at five sous a page.

And this life lasted for ten years.

At the end of ten years they had restored all, all, with interest of the usurer, and accumulated interest, besides.

Mme Loisel seemed old now. She had become a strong, hard woman, the crude woman of the poor household. Her hair badly dressed, her skirts awry, her hands red, she spoke in a loud tone and washed the floors in large pails of water. But sometimes, when her husband was at the office, she would seat herself before the window and think of that evening party of former times, of that ball where she was so beautiful and so flattered.

How would it have been if she had not lost that necklace? Who knows? Who knows? How singular is life and how full of changes! How small a thing will ruin or save one!

One Sunday, as she was taking a walk in the Champs Elysées to rid herself of the cares of the week, she suddenly perceived a woman walking with a child. It was Mme Forestier, still young, still pretty, still attractive. Mme Loisel was affected. Should she speak to

her? Yes, certainly. And now that she had paid, she would tell her all.

Why not?

She approached her. "Good morning, Jeanne."

Her friend did not recognize her and was astonished to be so

familiarly addressed by this common personage. She stammered:

"But, madame—I do not know—You must be mistaken."

"No, I am Matilda Loisel."

Her friend uttered a cry of astonishment: "Oh! my poor

Matilda! How you have changed."

"Yes, I have had some hard

days since I saw you, and some

miserable ones—and all because of

you."

"Because of me? How is

that?"

"You recall the diamond necklace that you loaned me to

wear to the minister's ball?"

"Yes, very well."

"Well, I lost it."

"How is that, since you returned it to me?"

"I returned another to you exactly like it. And it has taken us ten years to pay for it. You can understand that it was not easy for us who have nothing. But it is finished, and I am decently content."

Mme Forestier stopped short. She said:

"You say that you bought a diamond necklace to replace mine?"

"Yes. You did not perceive it then? They were just alike."

And she smiled with a proud and simple joy. Mme Forestier was touched and took both her hands as she replied:

"Oh, my poor Matilda! Mine were false. They were not worth over five hundred francs!"

❧